Zoey AND SASSAFRAS

GRUMPLETS AND PESTS

READ THE REST OF THE SERIES

TABLE OF CONTENTS

FOR NINA AND TIM — ML
FOR BUBS AND GOOSE (WITH AN ESPECIALLY BIG
SHOUT—OUT TO GOOSIE FOR GIVING ME THE CREATURE
NAME AND IDEA FOR THIS STORY!). — AC

Audience: Grades K-5.
LCCN 2019946195
ISBN 978-1-943147-67-0; ISBN 978-1-943147-68-7; ISBN 978-1-943147-69-4

Text copyright 2019 by Asia Citro
Illustrations copyright 2019 by Marion Lindsay
Journal entries handwritten by S. Citro

Published by The Innovation Press
1001 4th Avenue, Suite 3200 Seattle, WA 98154
www.theinnovationpress.com

Printed and bound by Worzalla
Production Date: June 2021 | Plant Location: Stevens Point, Wisconsin

Cover design by Nicole LaRue | Book layout by Kerry Ellis

PROLOGUE

These days my cat Sassafras and I are always desperately hoping we'll hear our barn doorbell.

I know most people are excited to hear their doorbell ring. It might mean a present or package delivery, or a friend showing up to play. But our doorbell is even more exciting than that. Because it's a *magic* doorbell. When it rings, it means there's a magical animal waiting outside our barn. A magical animal who needs our help.

My mom's been helping them basically her whole life. And now *I* get to help, too . . .

CHAPTER I
GROWING FOOD

"Blech!" Pip wrinkled his froggy nose as he poked at a leaf in my garden. "Humans really eat these things?"

I giggled and nodded. "Kale is totally delicious! My mom makes kale chips by tearing it up, adding a little salt, and baking it in the oven. They taste just like potato chips—yum!"

Pip narrowed his eyes at me. "Potatoes are also a weird thing to eat. Humans are so strange."

"Mrrowww?" Sassafras tapped a kale plant further down the row.

"Oh no, not you, too!" I scooted over and ruffled his fur. But he didn't look up at me. Instead he kept poking at a kale leaf. He sniffed at the leaf's underside and leapt backward.

"Oooh, what is that?" I touched what looked like a pile of tiny green dots on the bottom of my kale leaf. They moved. "Whoaaa!"

Sassafras started sneezing and snorting. He batted at his nose with his paws.

"Oh dear." I grabbed him and plucked a single green dot off his nose. I held it up to my face and squinted. "I see six legs! It must be some kind of insect?"

"Oooh, an insect?" Pip hopped over. "Finally, something delicious in your garden!"

"Ha," I said as I got down on my stomach to take a closer look at the kale leaf. "Nooo! There are a ton of tiny holes. These bugs are eating my kale!"

I tried shaking the leaf, and Sassafras tried batting at it, but the bugs stayed put.

"Allow me!" said Pip. He reached out, pulled off a bug, and popped it on his tongue. But then he made an "O" shape

with his mouth and his eyes crossed. "Ew! They're so sour!" He handed the wet bug back to me. "Sorry, Zoey."

"Um . . ." I wiped the slobbery bug on my pants. "Thanks for trying, Pip." I sat down with a big sigh. "We can't get them off—and there are so many! Apparently they're too gross to eat. But they're going to eat all of my kale if we don't do something!"

Pip patted my arm. "I'm sure you'll think of a plan, Zoey!"

I turned to Sassafras. "What do you think, Sass? Any ideas?" But he wasn't listening. He was looking off into the trees, ears twitching.

"Maybe Mom will know what—" I started to say before Pip shouted at me.

"Why did you even invite me over if you're just going to go back inside?!" He crossed his arms and scowled.

"Well, I—" But before I could finish, he kept on yelling!

"Your garden isn't fun, anyway! I'm tired of playing with you and Sassafras! I'm LEAVING!" He gave a big stomp and hopped off.

"Pip? Wait!" I called after him. But he didn't turn around.

"Well, that was weird," I said to Sassafras, but he was still super distracted.

I carefully plucked a tiny bug off the leaf to show my mom. I was almost to the house when I realized Sassafras wasn't following me.

"Are you coming, Sass?"

He looked between me and the forest, meowed, and then trotted inside with me.

CHAPTER 2
FARMER'S MARKET

Mom poked the bug with one finger. "Bummer. You've officially got your first garden pest!"

"Garden pest?" I asked. That sure didn't sound good.

"We aren't the only ones who like kale." Mom chuckled. "Slugs, snails, aphids–they're all creatures who can eat or damage your food before you get a chance to eat it. This little guy here is an aphid."

"But last year I didn't have any on my

kale! Did I do something wrong this year?"

"Not at all! Depending on the weather and predators and other things like that, you'll see more or less of certain pests each year. Last summer was pretty cool out—I bet it wasn't warm enough for the aphids."

My shoulders slumped. "Will there be any left by the time it's ready to harvest?"

"Are you guys ready for the market?" Dad called from the front door.

Mom gave my shoulders a squeeze. "Don't worry, sweetie. There are things we can do to help your plants. Let's figure it out after the farmer's market."

I nodded, but I didn't feel a whole lot better. It would be so unfair if all that time I'd spent growing the different plants from seeds was a waste because the aphids ate it up.

I was grumbly on the way to the market, but I cheered up once we got there. There were always so many fun foods to taste, and I liked finding weird vegetables and fruits to try.

I stood in front of my favorite fruit booth, trying to decide which sample to try first when two little arms wrapped around me and squeezed *really* tightly. Which could only mean . . .

"Sophie!" I squeaked.

Sophie laughed behind me and let go. I could breathe again! My friend could *definitely* give a tight hug. She'd make a good boa constrictor.

"Oh my gosh, Zoey, you have to come see this!" She grabbed my hand and dragged me to a new booth I hadn't seen before.

Sophie pointed to a container with weird black and orange bugs crawling around inside.

"GUESS! Guess what those are!"

"Ummm, some kind of beetle maybe?"

"They're BABY LADYBUGS!"

"No wayyy!" I peered closer. "Are you sure?"

"Aren't they neat?" A lady with a nametag that said "Nina" who was working at the booth smiled at us. "They look like skinny long beetles now. But after they shed a few times and grow, they'll pupate. And when they're done changing things up in there, perfect little ladybugs will come out!" She pointed to a pupa in the back of the container. It looked a little bit more like a ladybug—the right shape, anyway. "Do you like bugs?"

Sophie and I nodded furiously.

"Well, if you two garden at all, you'll love the bugs we have here today!" She waved her hand over some different containers.

"Ladybugs, lacewings, nematodes, and—oh, praying mantises!" I cheered. "I love those!"

"All of them eat garden pests, so they're pretty popular among organic gardeners. Do you guys know what organic gardening is?" Nina asked.

"It's when you grow your garden or food without using pesticide," Sophie said.

"Pesticides are bad for lots of creatures," I added. "Plus, if you use a lot of them, like on a farm, and it rains, they can get into local streams and really hurt the things that live there—like merhorses!"

Both Sophie and Nina stared at me.

"Mer-what?" Nina asked.

"Uhhh, I meant . . . mayflies!" Phew. That was a close one.

"Oh wow, you know about stream bugs?" Nina raised her eyebrows.

Sophie mumbled, "Merhorses?" and shook her head once.

"Pesticides can be bad for a lot of reasons—mayflies included!" Nina continued. "When you don't want to use pesticides, you have a few choices." She grabbed a jar and opened the lid and pulled out a HUGE green caterpillar.

"Whoaaa!" Sophie and I said at the same time.

Nina plonked the caterpillar in my hand. "Some pests, like this tomato hornworm or slugs, are big enough that you can pick them by hand."

I handed the caterpillar to Sophie so she could have a turn.

"If that isn't an option, another organic gardening method is planting a trap plant when you're making your garden." Nina lifted a flowering plant off the table.

"Nasturtiums!" I grinned. "I love eating those! The flowers are delicious!"

Nina laughed. "That's exactly how they work! If you plant them with your crop, often the pests will eat the nasturtiums instead."

I looked over the containers of insects. "So let's say you were growing kale, and you already planted it and there were a TON of aphids on it. Maybe some of these guys could save the day?"

"Exactly!" Nina said. "Ladybug larvae would be really helpful. And we're selling them today."

Sophie and I looked at each other and said, "Be right back!" at the same time.

We ran to get our parents from one of the fresh berry booths. I couldn't resist sneaking one sample raspberry before grabbing my mom's hand and telling her the great news. "Mom! Come see! I've got the solution for my garden pest problem right over here."

CHAPTER 3

PIP

Sophie and I sat cross-legged in my garden with two open containers of ladybug larvae between us.

"Whoa, look at the markings on this one!" Sophie held out her finger, and we oohed and aahed over the patterns on its back.

Sophie didn't have any aphids at her house, but she really wanted some of the ladybug larvae. So our parents decided that we could release both sets of larvae on my poor kale plants. They needed as much help as they could get.

A tiny orange paw darted toward one of the containers. "No way, buddy!" I scolded Sassafras.

"I still wish she had let me buy the tomato hornworm." Sophie sighed.

"But it's a PEST!" I reminded her.

"Yeahhh, I know. But it was so pretty! And also it grows into a moth." Sophie grinned. "I love moths."

I shuddered a little. I loved looking at moths from a distance. But their creepy Velcro-like feet and hairy-looking bodies freaked me out. Nina had showed us what kind of moth the tomato hornworm turned into. I was secretly glad that Sophie wasn't going to have that thing in her bedroom.

"Zoooeeyyy!" a little sing-songy voice called out. Sassafras bounded over to Pip who was walking out of the forest. "Oh, I didn't know you had company!"

Pip walked over and stood right in front of Sophie. Then he stuck out his tongue and made googly eyes at her.

Nothing.

Next he did a little tap dance.

Still nothing.

Pip laughed. "Oh, humans. They miss so much!"

I sighed. I kept hoping that one day Sophie would be able to see magical creatures. Of all of my friends, she'd be the

one. But still only my mom and I could see them. That meant I couldn't say anything to Pip with Sophie around, without seeming more than a little weird.

"Ummm, Sophie?" I asked. "I'm a little hungry—are you?"

"Oooh, snack time? Great idea!"

"Ummm . . ." I looked around for some kind of excuse. Aha! "Uh, I'm worried Sassafras will try to eat our larvae again. Would you go ask my parents for a snack? That way I can keep an eye on him."

"Oh, sure!" She set down the ladybug larva she'd been holding and ran across the yard to the house.

"Sorry about yesterday." Pip kicked at some dirt with his foot. "I guess I just had a really bad case of the grumplets."

I waited until Sophie was inside the house to reply. "Grumplets? Wait, do you mean a bad case of the grumpies?"

"What are grumpies?" asked Pip.

"What are grumplets?"

"I don't know—a grumpy forest creature?" Pip put a webbed finger to his chin. "It's a thing my mom and grandma used to say when I was little if I was too fussy."

"Huh. I've heard people say 'a bad case of the grumpies' when someone's grumpy. But I don't think they were talking about a forest creature."

Pip shrugged and peered into an open container of ladybug larvae. "Oooh, what are those?"

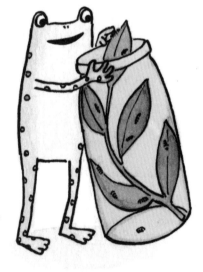

"Oh! They're baby ladybugs! I got them at the farmer's market. They're going to help by eating all those pesky aphids that are on my kale."

Pip shook his head. "I'm glad those things taste good to someone. Blech."

The back door swung open. "Sophie's coming back. Don't worry about earlier. We're all grumpy sometimes!"

"Thanks, Zoey." Pip gave my wrist a hug. "See you later!"

But he didn't go quite yet. He waited until Sophie sat down with our snack. Then he started cartwheeling away. "BYYYYEEEE SOOOPPHHHIIIEEE!" he

sang as he tumbled into the forest.

I couldn't help but giggle.

"What's so funny?" asked Sophie with a mouth full of strawberry.

"Uhh, I was just thinking how hilarious a cartwheeling frog would be," I said, grabbing a handful of delicious berries.

"That would be funny!" Sophie said and giggled, too.

CHAPTER 4

MERHORSES!

"Hey, cutie!" I said to the merhorse I held in my cupped hand underwater. I gently pet it with my thumb. Summer was such a great time to visit the merhorses because the creek water wasn't so freezing cold on my bare legs and hands! I'd been so busy with the aphids and kale that we hadn't gone to see the merhorses all week! Now that the ladybug larvae were on the job, I could finally take a break from the pests.

The merhorse batted its eyes and said something back to me, but without Pip here to translate, all I saw was bubbles. Oh well. I'm sure it said something nice.

"Isn't this one's mane so beautiful, Sassafras?" I moved my hands through the water toward where Sassafras was sitting. Only . . . Sassafras wasn't there anymore.

"Sass?" I turned around and saw his poof of a tail twitching a little ways behind me.

"What do you hear, buddy?" I strained my ears. Oh! Something was rustling—maybe a bird? It was making a weird noise. "What *is* that?"

I let the merhorse out of my hands to get a better view of Sassafras when the merhorse kicked me!

"OW!" I exclaimed. The happy-just-a-minute-ago merhorse pawed at my hands really hard with its front hoof. "Oh my goodness! What's the matter?"

It frowned and snorted. I quickly put it in the stream by another merhorse. Now I could hear even more of those weird noises behind me, but I wanted to make sure the merhorse I'd been holding was OK.

I grabbed my underwater viewer so I could see under the surface better. And oh gosh—the two merhorses were fighting! They were kicking at each other!

Over near some tall grass, Sassafras gave a loud "mrrowww!"

"One sec, Sass!" I called out. I used the viewer to look across the stream. The merhorses on the other side of the stream seemed fine. Maybe these two just didn't get along? Still . . . I'd never seen merhorses be anything but sweet to each other and to me.

Sassafras chattered. I looked up just as

he leapt over some grass and ran toward the trees. "Sassafras! Wait!" I dropped my underwater viewer and bounded after him.

He stopped a few feet away and sniffed at something in the sandy dirt. I crouched down and gave him a pet.

"Whoaaa!" I reached a hand out to touch what he'd found. "Those are some seriously weird footprints! What kind of creature left these?"

CHAPTER 5
FOOTPRINT

"Well, it sort of looked like, uh . . .
I mean, it had five toes. Or maybe six?
Ummm . . ." Uh-oh. Remembering the
footprint was hard now that it wasn't in
front of me.

Mom nodded and squinted and then
nodded some more. Then her eyes got
big and she held up a finger. "I've got an
idea!" she said and went to the craft supply
closet.

She set a big bucket labeled *Plaster of*

Paris on the kitchen table with a thud.

"Plaster?" I asked. "I don't want to do crafts right now. I want to figure out what that creature was."

"Oh, but that's exactly what we're going to do!" Mom said. "I'd come with you to see the footprint, but your dad might be a little suspicious if we both took off into the forest without inviting him along." She winked. "So I'll show you how to make a mold of the footprint you can bring back to show me."

"Whoaaa, cool!" I said. Sassafras, in his excitement, jumped onto the container. I grabbed him and sat with him in my lap on a kitchen chair.

"Okeydokey, let's see here," Mom mumbled as she grabbed a measuring cup and used it to fill a water bottle with two cups of tap water. Next she pulled out a big plastic ziplock bag and another measuring cup. She measured four cups of plaster of paris powder into the bag, then sealed it shut.

"When you get there, you'll need to find a bunch of small sticks and one big one."

"Sticks! Got it," I said.

"Use the small sticks to make a circle around the footprint. They'll help keep your plaster from flowing everywhere."

"Meow!" said Sassafras, and I nodded.

"Then take this water," she held up the water bottle, "and add it to this bag of plaster." She held up the ziplock bag as Sassafras touched his nose to it and stared inside. "Use the big stick to mix it until it's smooth. Then carefully pour it into the center of the footprint until you fill up the whole footprint right up to that stick border."

"OK, got it," I said. "Then what?"

"Then play for about thirty minutes. After that, check the plaster with your finger," Mom continued. "When it's hard to the touch, gently wiggle the plaster out of the ground and bring it home to dry overnight. After it's completely dry you can use a damp paper towel to clean off any remaining dirt."

A big grin spread across my face. "This is so cool!" I hopped up out of the chair and gave my mom a big hug. "Thank you!!!"

CHAPTER 6
MAKING A MOLD

Sassafras and I followed all my mom's steps to mix and pour the plaster. Now we were just waiting for it to dry.

In my earlier rush to get home, I guess I'd forgotten my underwater viewer by the stream.

"Whoops!" I said. I picked it up and peeked in at the merhorses. I found the one with the really pretty mane that had been so upset earlier. It was fine. No fighting.

Sassafras came over and bumped his

head into my leg. I scratched under his chin and he purred. "I guess that merhorse was feeling grumpy." I shrugged. "There must be something in the air—Pip was so grumpy yesterday, too. Huh."

I looked down at my cat, but he was staring at some grass that was moving nearby.

He chattered and his tail twitched.

Oh! Maybe the creatures who left the footprints were back!

I scooped him up and tiptoed closer. "Awww, it's just a sweet little bunny,

Sassafras," I whispered in his ear. He strained to get free. "No way, buddy. You are not going to chase that cute bunny!"

I held him a bit tighter and sat down quietly to watch the bunny. It took a giant bite of grass and then chewed and chewed and . . . Wait. Didn't it sound like a much quieter version of the sound I heard at the stream earlier? And the sound I heard in my garden with Pip? I closed my eyes and tried to remember.

"Oh gosh, Sassafras! I think that weird noise we keep hearing is CHEWING!"

In my excitement I'd forgotten to whisper. The poor bunny froze for a moment before bolting into the forest.

"Sorry, little guy," I whispered after him, then set Sassafras down.

I glanced at the bunny tracks just to be sure, but they looked like regular bunny tracks. So whatever was making that louder chewing noise was not a bunny. Or not a normal bunny, anyway.

Sassafras huffed and trotted over to the plaster mold. He pawed it once.

"Do you think it's ready?" I poked it with my finger. It seemed pretty solid. I wiggled it back and forth a few times, and it came free.

CHAPTER 7
CHEWING?

"Mooom!" I burst through the doorway and almost ran into her. "Oh, whoops! You're right there."

We both laughed.

I held out the footprint mold. "And whatever the creature is, it chews. At least, I'm pretty sure that's what those noises were. And there might have been a few of them—it sounded like more than one and there were a LOT of these footprints."

"Huh." Mom ran her finger along the

outline of the footprint. "This is going to sound strange, but what were your friends' moods like when you heard the creatures?"

"Both times they were SO grumpy! It was like, all of a sudden, too!"

Mom nodded. "Huh. So . . . years ago when I was much younger, I found a strange footprint in the forest. I think it looked like this one. I was so curious I asked two of my forest monster friends about it. One of them said it was a creature that makes everyone grumpy, and the other had a funny name for it. I should have written it down in my science journal!"

"OH! I think I know. Pip was talking about a grumpie. No . . . that's not quite it. Hold on a sec."

I dashed to my room, grabbed my Thinking Goggles, popped them on, and raced back to the kitchen.

"A bad case of the GRUMPLETS! That's what he said."

"Yes! That's it. That's what she called them—grumplets! But I haven't seen any footprints since then. I had forgotten about them until you showed me this." Mom handed the footprint mold back to me.

Mom put an arm on my shoulder. "Since the forest monsters seemed to know about them, I think your best bet is to go ask–"

"GORP!" we said at the same time.

Sassafras immediately started purring.

CHAPTER 8
FOREST MONSTERS

Sassafras and I didn't have to hike far before we heard the faint sound of music playing.

I grinned down at Sassafras. "Forest monster dance party!"

We ran into a clearing where a large group of young forest monsters were dancing to the music—including Gorp!

Sassafras, wild with happiness, bounced over to Gorp. He was purring SO loudly.

The young forest monsters spotted my cat and gasped. They huddled together on the other side of the clearing, shaking in fear.

Gorp stopped dancing and grimaced a bit. He reached out a finger gingerly and tapped Sassafras on the head.

A young monster screamed.

Sassafras fell over purring and rolled on the ground, begging for more pets from

Gorp.

Gorp called to his friends, "See? It's OK. He's a friend. He won't eat you, I promise!" He hesitated a moment, then reached out and tapped Sass once more.

Several monsters shook their heads. None of them came any closer.

Gorp gave me a big hug. "How are you? You and Sassafras out for a hike?"

"We came to see you!" I held out the plaster mold we'd made of the footprint. "Do you know what creature's footprint this is?"

Gorp turned it a few different ways before shaking his head and handing it back to me.

A few of his friends crept closer to get a better look, and I tilted the mold toward the brave monsters. "My mom and I think it might be a grumplet."

One of the monsters said, "I've heard about grumplets before!"

"You have?" I cheered and started

walking toward her. Which meant
Sassafras followed me.

The monster hid behind a friend.

"Oh, sorry!" I grabbed Sassafras and
took several steps back across the field.
"What do you know about them?" I called
over.

She peeked out from behind her
friend. After seeing that Sassafras was
restrained, she took a step closer and said,
"My grandma tells a story about them
when I'm in a bad mood. When she was a
little monster, they had the most perfect
summer—not too hot and not too cool.
But then the forest got a bad case of the
grumplets. Everyone fought and argued
instead of enjoying the wonderful weather.
Eventually when the seasons changed, the
grumplets moved on. So there was a happy
ending and all that."

"Hmmm . . ." I tapped my chin. "Maybe
the grumplets migrate with the seasons?"

Sassafras wiggled in my arms and

chattered at the group of monsters.

"Shhh, Sass! I know you want to love on the monsters but they're afraid!" I scolded.

One monster backed up to get farther away from Sassafras. A monster behind him shouted, "OUCH! You stepped on my foot!" and shoved him.

"It's not my fault you're ALWAYS IN MY WAY!" yelled the first monster and shoved him back. And just like that, all the monsters on the far side of the field were

pushing and shouting.

"UGH. You RUINED our dance party!" shouted the monster who'd been helping me.

"What?" I asked.

Gorp, who was standing closest to us, turned and headed over to the group of loud fighting monsters, calling, "You guys are being SO RUDE!"

I was so surprised by the whole thing that I loosened my grip on Sassafras. He wriggled out from my arms and bounded over to the grass behind the monsters.

They were so wrapped up in fighting that they didn't even notice my cat! "This has GOT to be the grumplets again," I whispered to myself and followed Sassafras on my tiptoes. Hopefully this time we'd get a peek at those troublemakers!

As I caught up to Sassafras, I heard the weird chewing sound again. Sassafras and I slowly parted the grass and saw a group of . . . grumplets? They were so little and cute I almost squealed, but I pressed my mouth shut, took a breath, and reminded myself that it might be my only chance to observe them. I needed to be a scientist and focus on gathering as much information as I could.

I couldn't see their feet through the grass, so I couldn't tell if they matched the footprint mold. I looked at their mouths. They were definitely chewing. It was the same sound from before. But what were

they eating?

I watched a grumplet that wasn't chewing step a bit closer to the monsters, then put a hand up in the air and wiggle its fingers. After a little wiggling, it reached up on its tippy toes and grabbed something. Then it pulled that thing into its mouth and began to chew. Another grumplet did the same. The more they pulled and chewed, the louder the fighting monsters got.

I leaned forward to see if I could tell what they were eating. Oh! Something seemed to shimmer in the light a little. Almost like a spiderweb? I leaned even farther forward and squinted my eyes. Yes! There were tiny, almost invisible, sparkly strands floating from the top of the monsters' heads over the grass and into the hands of the grumplets! I leaned a teeny bit farther forward to see better . . .

And then I fell.

With a very loud THUD.

CHAPTER 9
GRUMPLETS

I popped up just in time to see wide-eyed grumplets leaping backward and running off to the forest. As they turned to run, the airy, sparkly strings they'd been pulling on snapped and vanished. The grumplets were small, but they were FAST. There was no way Sassafras and I could catch up with them.

I sighed and brushed off my pants. My hand bumped the footprint mold in my pocket.

"Oh! We can at least see if their footprints are a match. Help me find some tracks, Sass!"

We hunted through the grass in opposite directions.

"Meow!"

Sure enough, my cat had found a patch of mud with some footprints in it. I held up the mold. It was an exact match.

I ruffled Sassafras's fur. "Great work!"

We turned back toward the clearing, but all the monsters were still fighting. So Sassafras and I trudged toward home. I hoped we could get to the bottom of this whole grumplet thing. If not, the summer was going to be LONG and frustrating, filled with grumpy, fighting magical friends! That would be such a bummer since the weather was so perfect for playing outside.

Back at home, I popped my Thinking Goggles on my head. "There must be some way to get the grumplets to leave."

I plopped down at the kitchen table. "OK. Let's write down what we know so far."

1. Grumplets have footprints that look like this: ✿

2. I think they eat something from my magical creature friends.

3. After they leave, my friends eventually feel better.

4. Grumplets seem to be scared of humans (or at least falling humans).

5. We think they migrate and will only be here during the summer.

6. They seem to only appear in years when the weather is just right.

I focused on what I saw while they were

chewing. They were taking something from my friends. And it was thin and sparkly. I tapped my fingers on the table. I thought I smelled popcorn. I looked around—no popcorn. "OK, Thinking Goggles, what does popcorn have to do with this?" I closed my eyes and thought of the last time I'd smelled popcorn like that. "The county fair! Oh! The popcorn machine was by the cotton candy machine. Oh! Oh! The sparkly strands from my friends looked just like cotton candy!" I clapped my hands.

Sassafras wove in between my legs.

"What could be coming from my friends that's like cotton candy, and losing it makes them grumpy?"

"Mrrowww?"

"Something . . . sweet . . . and happy. Wait." I scooped up Sassafras and put his forehead against mine. I looked into his eyes and asked, "Do you think it could be *joy*?"

CHAPTER 10

APHIDS

"Let's ask Mom, Sassafras!" I grabbed my science journal and peeked out the kitchen window and saw her in the garden.

Mom stood up and waved when she spotted us running toward her. "Hey, Zoey! Just the girl I wanted to see—look!" She pointed at my kale.

I bent down next to Sassafras who sniffed the leaf and purred. "Oh, wow! The aphids are almost gone. Thank goodness.

They were such PESTS!"

The Thinking Goggles suddenly felt tight on my head. "Oh my gosh! Mom! That's it! Maybe the grumplets are a forest pest! But instead of eating kale, they eat my magical friends' happiness! I saw them and–"

"You saw some grumplets?" Mom's eyes got wide.

"Yeah! They're really cute. Anyway,

I saw them pulling these weird sparkly strands, which looked like cotton candy, off my friends. Do you think that could've been their joy, Mom?"

"Interesting! That does sound like a good explanation to me. So, if you're right and they're pests eating something you don't want them to, what do you think we should do?" Mom tapped my science journal and winked at me.

I plopped down in the dirt and wrote in my journal while Sassafras chased a butterfly.

Ways to deal with grumplets:
1. Pesticides (No way).
2. Pick them by hand (Hahaha! I don't think I could catch them — and even if I could, where would I put them?)

3. Natural predator (Eek! They are annoying, but I don't want something to eat them!)

4. Trap plant

"Oh, that's a good idea!" I exclaimed. Mom smiled. "Tell me more!"

"Well, at the market, Nina said I could try a trap plant like nasturtiums for the aphids. A trap plant is basically something yummier than the plant they are attacking." I looked over and the butterfly had flown away, so now Sassafras was chasing a grasshopper. "OK . . . so if the grumplets want to eat my friends' happiness, what would taste better than that?"

I paced around the garden. "What tastes like happiness? Happiness . . . happiness . . ."

I tasted the sweetness of the cotton

candy from the fair on my tongue.
    "CANDY!"

CHAPTER 11
PIP (AGAIN)

"Why are you shouting about candy?" called a voice from the forest, and out hopped Pip.

"PIP!" Mom and I cheered.

"You were right," I told him. "Grumplets were making you grumpy the other day."

"I really did have a bad case of the grumplets?" Pip asked.

"Yep!" I nodded. "Sassafras and I saw them causing trouble with the forest monsters yesterday. I'm pretty sure they're eating all the happiness from magical creatures."

Pip wrinkled his nose. "Happiness is another weird thing to eat." Then he shrugged. "Makes more sense than kale, though."

I rolled my eyes. "I think if we can get them to eat candy instead, they'll leave you guys alone!"

Dad peeked into the kitchen and called, "Hey, honey?"

Mom patted my head. "It sounds like you guys have this handled. Tell me what you learn later!" She sneaked Pip a quick kiss and headed into the house.

Pip touched his cheek and smiled, then turned back to me. "So, how do we get them to eat candy instead?"

"Hmmm . . ." I said. "Oh! Are you willing to help me try something?"

"Of course!" he replied.

"Great—you two wait here, and I'll be right back."

Once I filled my backpack with all the stuff I needed, I set out for the meadow where the monsters had been fighting earlier. I told Pip my plan along the way.

When we got there, I laid out a little napkin as a frog-sized picnic blanket and handed Pip a small bag of chocolate candy. Then I scooped up Sassafras and hid in the bushes at the edge of the field.

"OH, THIS IS SOOO GOOD!" Pip shouted as loudly as he could while pretending to eat a bite of candy.

He looked around. Nothing. "I AM SO, SO, SO HAPPY RIGHT NOW!" he shouted again while taking a fake bite.

"I AM JUST OOOZING HAPPINESS RIGHT NOW. JUST SO MUCH HAPPY RIGHT HERE IN THIS MEADOW!"

I sighed. Maybe this wasn't going to work. Grumplets might not understand what he was saying. Or they might be on the other side of the forest. Or . . .

"Mrrowww!" Sassafras's ears pricked

toward Pip.

I leaned forward (but not too much this time) and saw the grass on the other side of Pip rustling. "Yesss!" I whisper-shouted. "Grumplets!"

But then Pip frowned and stood up. "THIS WAS A TERRIBLE IDEA."

Oh no. A grumplet scampered close to Pip. It wiggled its fingers and started pulling and chewing. Other grumplets joined in. They were eating Pip's happiness!

"UGH. IT'S NOT EVEN WORKING," Pip yelled as he threw the bag of candy on the ground. The candies rolled out, and one landed at the feet of a grumplet.

I held my breath.

The grumplet looked down and poked the candy with its toe. Then it reached down for the candy. It held it up. Sniffed it. Sneezed. And then . . . IT ATE THE CANDY!

The grumplet rubbed its tummy and took a few more steps into the clearing

and found another candy. And ate it. A nearby grumplet let go of a strand of Pip's happiness and walked over to a candy and ate it. Another grumplet did the same.

"YOU ARE NO FUN TO PLAY WITH, ZOEY!" Pip stomped once and then hopped off.

Sassafras struggled to get free to go after Pip but I held him tight. I whispered in his ear, "They didn't see the candy right away, but look!"

All of the grumplets were now eating candy. It was working!

CHAPTER 12
CANDY

Back at the house, I sat at the kitchen table and wrote in my science journal:

I think candy can work like a ~~trap plant~~ for grumplets!

Sassafras jumped up and snuggled into my lap.

"OK, I think it could work! We just need to put candy in the forest. Or … give our friends candy to throw when they start feeling grumpy? Or … ?" I looked down at Sassafras.

He bumped my chin with his head. "Meow."

"Yeah, there's no way we can actually use candy. It would get all gross in the forest. It works, but it's still not actually a solution. Great." I crossed my arms on the table and lay my head down.

"Hey, kiddo!" I felt a hand on my head.

"Hey, Dad," I grumbled.

"It sounds like you could use a snack, huh?"

"Mrrowww!" Sassafras leapt down from my lap and wove between my dad's legs.

Dad laughed and went to the fridge.

"OK, buddy, a snack for you too."

When I heard the sound of a plate being set in front of me, I finally lifted my head. "Thanks."

He frowned. "You OK?"

"Yeah." I leaned my head on my hand. "Just stuck on a problem."

"Want any help?"

"I'm sure I'll figure it out eventually," I said. And then I crossed my fingers under the table because I really hoped I was right about that.

Dad grabbed a can of cat food from the pantry. I heard the grating sound of the electric can opener whirring.

Sassafras also heard it, and began prancing with joy.

At least someone was happy. "Ugh. Why can't I just plant candy!?!" I exclaimed. I popped a strawberry in my mouth.

Dad chuckled. "Good one, Zoey! Plant candy!"

"Huh?" I said through a mouthful of

berry.

"Isn't that what you said?" Dad set Sassafras's snack down. "I couldn't hear over the can opener. I thought you called your berries 'plant candy,' which is pretty clever! I mean, they are sort of exactly that, right?"

Plant candy! That was it!!! I leapt up and gave him a big squeeze. "You're a genius, Dad!"

"Uh, thanks?" said Dad with one eyebrow raised as he headed back to his office.

A head peeked in the kitchen. "What

did I miss?" asked Mom.

I gave her a quick summary of
everything I'd figured out.

"Interesting hypothesis!" she said.
"What are you going to do next?"

Hmmm. I looked at the notes in my
science journal. "Well, I think I'll try what I
did last time with Pip, but maybe this time
I'll have him throw the food toward the
grumplets from the start. That way maybe

they'll eat the berries right away and leave Pip's happiness alone!"

"That sounds like a great plan," said Mom.

"Meow!" added Sassafras.

"Oh! And if that works, then we need to find berries in the forest. Or could we plant them in a part of the forest farther away? The monsters said the grumplets eventually move on to other places. Maybe if we get them to start heading somewhere else, we can have the rest of the summer to play without grumpiness!"

Sassafras purred.

"I'll get Pip to run another test with me, but this time with berries," I said. "While we do that, could you figure out if there's a patch of forest berries somewhere at the edge of the forest away from my friends?"

Mom smiled. "I'd be happy to."

"All right, Sass, let's go find—" I was about to say "Pip" when the magic doorbell rang.

Sassafras and I exchanged a look and ran off to the barn.

CHAPTER 13
PIP (AGAIN, AGAIN)

I wondered if we would find a new magical creature in trouble. Or maybe someone else had noticed the grumplets were making everyone in the forest miserable and had come to us for help?

I opened the door, and there was Pip.

"Sorry about earlier when I threw the candy, Zoey," he said, looking at the ground instead of at me. "I just had a—"

"BAD CASE OF THE GRUMPLETS!" we said at the same time and laughed.

"It's OK, Pip. We understand," I said as Sassafras, Pip, and I shared a three-way hug.

"Have you come up with a solution yet?" Pip asked. "It's getting really bad out there in the forest. EVERYONE is fighting. I'm having the worst summer ever."

"Don't worry, Pip. I've got a plan."

Pip was excited to help, so after I grabbed my bowl of berries, his napkin picnic blanket, and my science journal, he hopped on my head and the three of us headed out to the clearing once again.

We got Pip all set up, and Sassafras and I once again hid in the bushes.

"OH, THESE BERRIES ARE SO DELICIOUS!" Pip proclaimed.

"THEY TASTE LIKE HAPPINESS AND JOY AND JUST SO MUCH GOODNESS!"

He waved his arms about.

"I JUST DO NOT HAVE THE WORDS TO DESCRIBE THEIR YUMMINESS. EVERYONE SHOULD TRY THESE! HAPPY! JOY!"

Sassafras's ears pricked. The grumplets came faster this time! I quietly clapped my hands.

I gasped. "Sass—look!" I whisper-shouted to my cat. "They are looking on the ground first!"

Sure enough, instead of grabbing the

joy in the air first, the grumplets were snorting and snuffling along the ground.

Pip started flinging berries every which way. "OH, WHOOPS! I'M SUCH A SLOPPY EATER! BERRIES ARE GOING EVERYWHERE!"

I held my hand over my mouth while I laughed. Oh, Pip!

It worked, though. The grumplets made their way over to the berries Pip had tossed everywhere and ate them!

"OH MY, I AM RUNNING OUT OF BERRIES! UHHH . . . ?" Pip gave me a worried look.

Oh no! Would those berries be enough for the grumplets to leave Pip's joy alone?

He tossed around the final few, and we all waited. I was sure that he'd storm off at any minute. But then a weird thing happened. The grumplets patted their tummies. And then walked away.

After they were gone, Pip hopped over to us. "Zoey! It worked! I don't feel the least bit grumpy!"

"WE DID IT!" Pip and I cheered and hopped up and down while Sassafras bounded around us.

It was time to try the last part of my plan.

CHAPTER 14
THE BIG PLAN

"MOOOM!" I shouted as I came through the back door with a frog on my head and a cat at my feet.

Mom grinned as soon as she saw our happy, excited faces. "It worked!"

"It totally did," I said. "Pip didn't even get grumpy. The grumplets got full on berries just as we ran out of them. It was a close call."

Pip hopped over to my mom's shoulder and gave her a snuggle. "So now we need to find a big patch of strawberries in the forest, right?"

Mom had him hop onto her hand so she could talk to him better. "Well, not exactly. We don't have any wild strawberries growing around here."

"Oh," said Pip, thinking for a moment. "Then let's plant some blackberries!"

"Well," said Mom, "blackberries are actually invasive plants around here."

"Invas-a-what?" asked Pip.

"Invasive means that it grows too much in a place it's not supposed to," I chimed in. "Then there's no room for the native plants—the plants that are supposed to be here."

Pip flopped down on my mom's palm. "Well then, that's it. We're DOOMED."

Mom and I laughed.

"Don't give up yet, Pip!" Mom lifted his chin with her finger. "I found a local reforestation group that's doing some native plantings a few miles away in a nearby forest."

"YESSS!" I pumped my fist. "Berries too?"

"They are planting a bunch of different things," Mom said. "Some are trees, some are bushes, and some are definitely berries. They said they had several black-capped raspberries, huckleberries, and thimbleberries that need to be planted."

My tummy rumbled, and Mom and I

laughed. "I love forest berries," I told Pip. "A lot."

"I signed us up for the planting this Saturday," Mom said. "It's summer, so the berry plants we're planting should be producing berries right now. But . . ."

"We have to find a way to get the grumplets over to the new patch of berries after we plant them," I finished.

"Exactly," said Mom.

My shoulders dropped. "There's no way Pip could yell about how tasty the berries are from miles away."

"That's true." Pip grinned. "But you know someone who is loud enough." He held out his hand, waiting for me to figure it out.

I knew someone who could yell from miles away? But to be that loud they'd have to be seriously HUGE. "OH!" I gasped.

Mom raised her eyebrows at me. She still hadn't guessed.

"Tiny!" I cheered.

CHAPTER 15

TINY!

On Saturday, Mom and I worked *hard* with the team of volunteers planting the native plants, including all the berries. But I didn't mind the work. I love plants, and even better than that—the next day I was going to see TINY!!! I hadn't seen him since I helped heal his hoof.

"Do you think he'll be even bigger?" I whispered to Mom as we patted down the soil around a thimbleberry we'd just planted.

"I suspect so." Mom laughed. "Though

that's hard to imagine, isn't it?"

I grinned. I could hardly wait.

After we got home and washed up, I did my best to keep busy. I read books, brushed Sassafras, checked on my garden, and finally went to sleep. I dreamed of unicorns, obviously.

The next morning, Mom and Sass and I took the car to the new berry patch. As we turned the corner and it came into view, I pressed my whole face against the window.

"WHOAAA!" I said.

Six ginormous unicorns towered over everything. I squinted at their hooves. Oh! There was our tiny Pip!

We parked, and Sassafras and I burst out of the car and ran over to Tiny, who was, in fact, taller.

"ZOEY AND CAT!!!" Tiny boomed.

"Tiny!" I hugged his enormous leg while Sassafras lovingly rubbed his face on another leg.

Tiny tilted his head one way and said,

"TINY'S MOM AND DAD!" and then tilted it the other way and said, "TINY'S SISTER AND BROTHERS."

"It's so nice to meet you all!" I shouted up. Each member of Tiny's family took turns lowering their heads so I could pet them gently on the nose.

"UNICORNS HAPPY TO HELP," Tiny said. "MUCH GRUMPY IN THE FOREST. ZOEY FIX IT?"

"I sure hope so. Let's get these grumplets out of our forest!"

The unicorns nodded. The gust of wind

knocked me down, and Pip and Sassafras
went rolling.

"OOPS. SORRY!" said the unicorns.

Pip brushed himself off, and Sassafras
gave a good shake. "Let's stick to 'yes' or
'no' instead of nodding, yeah?" Pip said.

"YES," said the unicorns.

"OK," Pip continued, "Zoey and I are
going to make a trail of berries from the
edge of the forest over to this new patch
of berries. Once we've set that down, we
need you to shout about how good the
berries are. Hopefully the grumplets will

come running toward your voices, find the berry trail, and follow it to our new field of berries. Got it?"

"YES," said the unicorns.

Mom handed me and Pip each a container of berries. We didn't want to use up the wild ones growing on the bushes for this. Then we laid out a trail of berries leading from the edge of the forest over to the new patch of berries. I crossed my fingers, whispered, "please let this work," and then nodded up to the unicorns as everyone on the ground covered their ears with their hands.

"NEW GOOD BERRIES!" shouted one.

"MANY KINDS OF YUMMY," shouted a second.

"WE HAVE MUCH HAPPY OVER HERE!" added Tiny.

We waited and waited. The unicorns used their loudest voices to let the whole forest know about the new berries.

But where were the grumplets?

CHAPTER 16
DISAPPOINTED

I dragged my feet over to Mom. "I don't understand. I thought this would work!" I felt like crying, but I took some breaths and tried to stay calm. We'd figure out something, I told myself.

"I did too, sweetie." Mom hugged me. "But it's a long way to walk. First the grumplets have to hear the unicorns, then they have to walk a few miles through the forest toward the sound until they find the berry trail from the edge of the forest to here. That could take some time, I imagine."

"I guess," I said. "It's just that the grumplets were really fast when I saw them last. I figured they'd be here by now." I flumped to the ground, crossed my legs, and set my head in my hands. Pip and Sassafras came over and snuggled me.

Then Sassafras started chattering.

I looked up. Sassafras was chattering? That meant . . .

"Yesss!" I whispered. I could see the first of the grumplets eating a berry from our berry trail.

The unicorns spotted it and stopped shouting. They effortlessly glided to either side of the berry trail to clear a path for the grumplets.

First one, then another, then several more grumplets appeared. They followed the berry trail just like I'd planned.

When the grumplets got to the plants, they looked a little confused. Then they started snuffling. One found a berry on the plant and stared for a minute, then plucked it off and ate it.

The others watched and did the same!

"I hope there are enough berries!" I whispered to Mom, and she nodded.

They ate just a few of the wild berries before patting their stomachs. The smallest grumplet gave a little burp!

"What are they going to do now, Zoey?" whispered Pip.

"I have no idea," I whispered back.

The grumplets moved a bit farther into the new patch of plants, and one of the grumplets pointed at an old hollowed-out tree trunk. All the grumplets snortled and squeaked at each other, and then they looked along the ground.

I stood and picked up Sassafras so we could get a better view. Pip hopped on Mom's head and she stood too.

"What are they doing?" I whispered.

The grumplets were gathering up moss and lichen and putting it in the hollow part of the trunk.

"Oh! I think they are making a bed!" I quietly told Sassafras.

"Meow!" he replied.

One by one the grumplets piled on top of each other inside the tree trunk. Before we knew it, they were SNORING! We held back our giggles so we wouldn't wake them.

CHAPTER 17
TIME TO CHECK

Mom said there was no telling what the grumplets would do next—we just had to wait and hope.

Sassafras and I did our best to keep busy. We went on a lot of hikes, built forts, had playdates with friends, made kale chips, and crafted.

It was getting hotter and hotter, so we went to the stream to cool off. I eagerly rolled up my pants and waded into the stream. The merhorses chased me and licked my ankles, which made me crack up. Sassafras was, of course, staying dry on the shore, watching us play.

"Hey, Sassafras!" I said between fits of laughter. "It's been a long time since any of our friends have been *really* grumpy."

"Meow!" he exclaimed. He turned to chase a cricket in the grass.

"Do you think Mom will drive us out to check on the grumplets yet?" I asked him as I smiled down at the merhorses in the water.

"Mrrowww," he said, distracted by the cricket chase, followed by a much louder "MEOW!"

That couldn't be good.

I looked over to see Sassafras giving Pip an angry look.

"Ah, crickets are delicious." Pip rubbed his belly. "Sorry, old friend."

I shuddered, thinking of how crunchy crickets must be. Ew.

"Hey, Zoey!" Pip called. "I thought I

heard you laughing. I wanted to ask you—
are the grumplets officially gone? No one's
seen them in the forest lately."

I wiggled my fingers underwater
to wave goodbye to the merhorses and
carefully waded over to the shore. "We
were just talking about asking Mom if
she'd drive us over to check. Want to
come?"

Pip hopped up on my head, and I took

him and Sassafras across the stream and back to my house. We all pleaded with Mom until she agreed to take us.

We were just getting in the car when I remembered my camera. "One sec!" I said and dashed off to get it.

Once we got to the berry patch, we noticed there were a few ripe ones that were uneaten. "That's a good sign, right?" I asked. "Maybe they've already moved on."

"Could be," Mom said, fanning herself.

We peeked in the hollow tree trunk. It looked like it had been slept in, but we couldn't see or hear the grumplets anywhere.

"Mrrowww!" called Sassafras from farther away.

We followed the sound, and I squatted down next to him. "What did you find, buddy?"

Sassafras put his nose to a patch of what had once been mud. I brushed aside some grass and branches and sure

enough—we saw grumplet footprints that
the heat had dried into the mud.

"Mom!" I exclaimed. "These are leading
away from the forest, right? Do you think the
grumplets have moved on? Maybe they're
looking for more berries farther away?"

"It looks like it!" Mom gave me a high-
five.

I reached into my backpack and pulled
out my camera. "I forgot to take a photo

when the grumplets were around. Do you think you could get a photo of us by the grumplet footprints for my science journal?"

Mom took the camera, and Pip and Sassafras and I gathered around the footprints and grinned.

At home, as I went to put the photo into my science journal, I noticed a sweet smell. "No way," I said to myself as I tilted the photo left, then right. Yep. I could just barely make out the sparkly strands of Pip's joy floating around him.

After I glued down the scented photo, I opened my science journal to a new blank page so it was ready for the next magical creature we would meet.

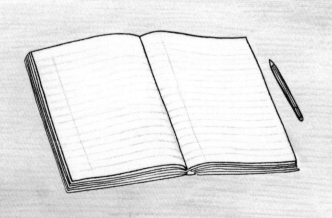

GLOSSARY

Aphid: A small insect that feeds on sap from plants and damages them.

Larva: The baby form of an insect that goes through metamorphosis (which means it looks very different at different ages).

Migration: When a living thing moves from one place to another based on the seasons (temperatures).

Pest: An animal or insect that damages another animal or plant.

Pesticide: A chemical that kills pests but is often harmful to other animals (including people!).

ABOUT THE AUTHOR AND ILLUSTRATOR

ASIA CITRO used to be a science teacher, but now she plays at home with her two kids and writes books. When she was little, she had a cat just like Sassafras. He loved to eat bugs and always made her laugh (his favorite toy was a plastic human nose that he carried everywhere). Asia has also written three activity books: *150+ Screen-Free Activities for Kids, The Curious Kid's Science Book,* and *A Little Bit of Dirt.* She has yet to find a baby dragon in her backyard, but she always keeps an eye out, just in case.

MARION LINDSAY is a children's book illustrator who loves stories and knows a good one when she reads it. She likes to draw anything and everything but does spend a completely unfair amount of time drawing cats. Sometimes she has to draw dogs just to make up for it. She illustrates picture books and chapter books as well as painting paintings and designing patterns. Like Asia, Marion is always on the lookout for dragons and sometimes thinks there might be a small one living in the airing cupboard.

for activities and more visit
ZOEYANDSASSAFRAS.COM